α T

/

raz temani
18/03/06

My Alien Penfriend

By

Faiz Kermani

1663 LIBERTY DRIVE, SUITE 200
BLOOMINGTON, INDIANA 47403
(800) 839-8640
WWW.AUTHORHOUSE.COM

First published by AuthorHouse 10/10/05

ISBN: 1-4208-5860-2 (sc)

*Printed in the United States of America
Bloomington, Indiana*

This book is printed on acid-free paper.

For Nathalie

Location: London, England
Planet: Earth
Date: 35th January 2286

Dear Zmod

Guess what? I'm your new penfriend! I was sent your spacemail address by the Inter-Galactic space club. I've been a member of the club for two months now and I've had great fun making friends in different parts of the universe. You're the first person from Bartoch that I've sent a spacemail to - I can't wait to learn about your planet!

My name is Darius Chevalier and I am from Earth. I am 11.4 solar cycles old, but soon I will be 12. I live in a city called London in the country of England, which is in the north of the planet. I live at home with my father and my mother. I also have an older sister called Sirah - she is studying Cosmic Architecture at university.

We also have a pet dog called Ranger. My sister bought him for me on my 8th birthday. When I come home from school I like to take him for walks. There is a big park at the back of our house and Ranger likes to run around there and chase other dogs. He is a German shepherd and so he is a bit crazy!

I am still at school. It's called Jupiter Secondary and it is in the centre of London.

My favourite lessons at school are Atomic Science and Galaxy History. I really like studying about other planets and so I am happy to be writing to you. In my Science lesson the other day, our teacher told us that on

Bartoch the sky is green and that there are two moons. Is that true? What are they like? I can't imagine there being two moons around the Earth.

Galaxy History lessons are really fun. Our teacher is very funny and he knows lots of interesting stories about people who lived in the olden days. Sometimes he takes us on school trips to history museums so that we can learn more about what life used to be like on different planets in the past. Recently, we started studying about the first attempts from our planet to colonise the moons of Jupiter. The spaceships look very old and strange looking. It makes me laugh to think that people used to think that they were modern!

The lesson I hate the most is Stellar Mathematics – it's boring! My father keeps telling me that it will be very important for me to know when I grow up, but at the moment I don't understand why we have to learn it. There are so many things to remember and I always get them wrong! I wish we only had to study the things we liked at school. It's a waste of time studying boring subjects.

I suppose that you are still at school as well. I would like to know about your school and which lessons are your favourite. Do you ever learn about our planet? What do people on Bartoch think about Earth?

I have a lot of hobbies. I like to make model spaceships and fly them. Sometimes my father helps me. When I take Ranger for a walk in the park I sometimes climb onto a tree and try to launch the models I make. Unfortunately, most of them don't fly very far, but Ranger always brings them back to me if they crash !

I also love to play sports. My favourite is football. Do you know this sport on Bartoch? I play every weekend in a local team. Our team is quite good. This year we are hoping to win some competitions.

Well, I can't wait for you to write to me and tell me about your planet. I hope we can become really good friends.

Bye for now!
Darius

4

Make new friends from other planets through the Inter-Galactic Space Club !

Joining our penfriend club is a fantastic way to make new friends across the universe. Just send your name, spacemail address and a payment of 20 electronic Earth credits to:

Mr. Norbert Alia
Organiser
The Inter-Galactic Space Club
Spacemail Box E5X2i
London, England

Once we've received your details we'll send you a special password so that you can access the Members Section of our special intergalactic computer. In the Member's Section you'll find all the instructions you need to create a page that only you can access. As soon as you've done this, you can begin spacemailing the penfriend of your choice!

Your spacemails will be translated and then transmitted electronically to the club computers on other planets twice every month. What's even better is that you'll never lose your penfriend's replies as their messages will be stored permanently in the Member's section. Log on as frequently as you like and write to as many people as you like!

So what have you got to lose? Get writing now! With over 10 trillion penfriends from over 300 different planets you'll never be short of friends again!

Location: Vakpak, Bozkin
Planet: Bartoch
Date: 29th Girion, Hexile 14783

Dear Darius

Thanks for your spacemail. I was really excited when it arrived on my computer! I've never spacemailed anyone from Earth! Like you I also hope that we can become good friends.

Did you have any problems in getting access to the club's computer? At first my password didn't work. I could only read your spacemail but I couldn't send a reply. Anyway, I managed to contact their local office. They were very helpful. Once they gave me a new password, everything worked perfectly. It's pretty easy isn't it? I don't really understand how they manage to transmit the messages through the time-space interface, but I'm glad that the system is so fast. Otherwise we would probably have to wait many stellar orbits for an answer.

I am 15 stellar orbits old – I think it's similar to your age. How tall are you? I am now 86 mariqions. I am the smallest in my class at school.

My full name is Zmod Tarib. I live with my parents and my pet glod, Darak. Do you know what a glod is? They have four legs and a hairy tail. Darak has blue fur. My uncle gave him to me when I was four stellar orbits old. I like his bubbles. He is my best friend!!!

We live in Vakpak – not too far from the centre. Do you know that it's the capital city of the country of Bozkin ? I suppose you don't hear much about our country on your planet. Let me explain.

Bozkin is a country in the south of the planet. My father is from Bozkin, but my mother comes from another country called Tarzak. Sometimes we go there for our holidays to see my aunts and uncles and cousins. I like Tarzak because we can go above ground more than here. Do you live above ground ?

I am in class 10 at Jellibech Springs College and I really like it there. It is named after some famous springs nearby which produce lots of hot neon. Some people are scared because there is also a volcano called the Arqiat Crater near our school. It's actually very safe. The last time that it erupted was over a thousand hexicycles ago, so I hope that we are OK!

My favourite lesson at school is Protection of the Ground studies. I also like Astronomic Geography. Our teacher, Mr. Garbur, knows a lot about Earth. He told us that as part of his university course he visited Earth. He likes to tell us stories about his time there. Can you tell me more about the countries on your planet? Are there really 543?

By the way, you're right - on Bartoch the sky is green except for at the East pole and West pole where it is red. My grandfather used to be a geologist. He told me that at the Bartochian poles the sky is red because light from the sun passes through lots of dust created by meteors. It's also true that we have two moons – let me explain.

The two moons are known as Alyannah and Variel. It's very weird because Variel is not actually a real moon. We learned that many centuries ago it was a planet, but it was destroyed because of earthquakes. Sometimes people call it the 'dead planet', even though

I don't know if anyone actually died. It's a bit of a scary story! Our teacher told us that it became trapped near the atmosphere of Bartoch. As it appears in our sky at night, people simply call it a moon.

My father is a commander in the engineering corps of the army. His base is in the west of Vakpak, but I am not allowed to go there because it is only for people who are in the army. Sometimes though they have a party for the families of all the people who work at the base. I like going to these parties - they take us flying in different hoverjets through the caves!

My mother works as a nurse at the local hospital. She often works during the night. Sometimes she is very tired. At the beginning I didn't really like going into the hospital. It scared me a bit because everyone there was ill. Then my mother told me that I shouldn't be worried because the people are there so that they can become better. Now I find it interesting because my mother shows me how they cure people using different medicines.

I have lots of hobbies too. I like to collect rocks – especially moving ones - from different places. I have an electron database that shows the different types of rock found on Bartoch and where they came from. At the moment I have over 100 rocks. Most of them come from volcanoes. My ambition is to find a meteor, like my grandfather did in the East Pole. They burn up in the atmosphere after they have flown through space. They are very rare.

After school Darak and I often go to hunt for rocks in the tunnels around our house. Darak is really good at chasing the moving ones! Yesterday we caught three of them! It's amazing that we found so many. Darak knows when I have spotted a moving rock because he bounces to the opposite side so that we can prevent it from escaping. Then he screeches at it until it stops moving. The rocks we found yesterday were blue and were quite noisy. I think that they must have originally come from the centre of Bartoch. They must have climbed for many stellar orbits to reach our tunnel!

It is strange that you still actually play sports on Earth! Why? On Bartoch we stopped doing that a long time ago ~ computers can do everything now, so what is the point ? I am a member of a special games club, which connects many of the computers on the planet. I like to play against players in different countries. The club is always bringing out new games, so we never get bored!

I have heard about football, but I don't know much about it. What happens when you play it?

Well it is really late now and I must go and do my homework. I have a stellar maths assignment to finish. I need to start it now. It is very difficult so I might have to get my father to help me.

Please spacemail soon – or as we say here in Bozkin "Clotpid huy pek!" I am looking forward to hearing more about your life on Earth.

May peace be granted to you!
Your friend
Zmod

Darius was excited. He was in contact with someone from a different planet! At first he had been nervous about joining the Inter-Galactic Space Club, but his mother had insisted. She had said that it might be a way of stopping him from getting bored. She had a point - Darius became bored easily. There was nothing that annoyed his family more than to see him wandering around the house claiming that he had nothing to do.

Darius looked up at his space chart. Bartoch was so far away. He wondered how long it would take before Zmod would read his spacemail. Maybe a couple of weeks because they had to be translated before they could be sent electronically? Then he would have to wait for a similar amount of time to get a reply. What would Zmod write? It was fascinating to hear about life on Bartoch.

Perhaps one day in the future he would be able to visit Zmod. That would be fun. As he closed his eyes and drifted off to sleep, he imagined that he was about to embark on a journey to Bartoch.

Location: London, England
Planet: Earth
Date: 29th February 2286

Dear Zmod

Thanks a lot for your spacemail! It is really exciting to be in contact with you! I was very interested in all the things you wrote about life on Bartoch. It's going to be a lot of fun to see what is similar and what is different on our two planets!

You asked me how tall I am - I am now 1 metre 10 centimetres. I suppose that it's not very big - there are quite a few people who are taller than me in my class. My mother tells me not to worry and that I will grow a lot taller later on - she says that most people in my family are tall. I suppose she is right because my father is taller than most of the other parents who come to collect their children at my school.

I am glad that you are learning about Earth. You asked me about the different countries we have – I had to look in my electronic encyclopaedia for the information! Apparently we now have 541 countries on our planet – I believe two small ones were taken over last week, but I don't remember their names. It's funny because I didn't actually know we had so many countries - there are a lot of small countries I have never heard of before! I know that our planet is ruled by a government called the World War Council and that each country sends someone to it. Once the English Ambassador came to our school to give a talk about the World War Council. I know it's important for us to know these things, but it was actually quite a boring talk! From what I understand the World War Council doesn't seem to work that well anyway.

We've only recently started learning about your planet in our astronomy class. I didn't realise that you had to live underground! That must be really weird! Do you have light down there?

I was surprised that people on Bartoch don't play sports now. It's true that computers and machines can do many things, but we still like to play games. It helps keep us fit and it's good fun to run about outside.

By the way, football is a really exciting sport - I am sure that you would like it! I'll try to explain it to you but it would be much easier if I could show you! Basically, you have three teams of five people. Each team protects a set of metal poles on a triangular field from being hit by two round objects called balls. The winner is the team that manages to hit the poles as many times as possible during the match. Usually what teams try to do is eliminate the strongest team first so that they only have to worry about each other at the end. You have to be careful though because sometimes a team pretends to make an alliance with you to destroy the strong team and then they suddenly attack you!

Your glod sounds really funny! Why does he make bubbles? Is it very common to own a glod on your planet? Are they all blue? On Earth, dogs are kind of rare nowadays, because of the Great Canine Death of 2098. I am really lucky to have Ranger! I try to take him for a walk every day after I come back from school because if I don't take him out he gets very grumpy and starts making a lot of noise! Yesterday when I came back home it was raining but he still wanted to go out. I didn't really want to go, but my mother told me that I had to. It was horrible because I got completely wet! By the way, on Earth rocks cannot move on their own. I would love to see a moving rock from your planet!

How did you do with your Stellar Maths assignment? Tomorrow is the day I hate the most at school because my first lesson is Maths.

I hope you'll spacemail me soon again. I am really looking forward to your message.

Your friend
Darius

Location: Vakpak, Bozkin
Planet: Bartoch
Date: 14th Harcifion, Hexile 14783

Dear Darius

Thank you for your spacemail. I enjoy writing to you! I am glad that you like to hear about life on my planet. I really enjoy hearing about what Earth is like.

You have a lot of countries on your planet! We have only 18! On Bartoch our system is very different to yours because we don't have governments any more. Now the Mind Complex controls everything on our

planet. Let me try to explain because only special people can join it. They have to be selected first. It's a really good system because there are a lot less problems like wars and pollution than before. Two stellar orbits ago, one of my father's cousins was selected for the Mind Complex. It was so exciting because we got to go to his admission ceremony. When they fused his mind to the others in the Complex, I got a little scared, but it was an incredible experience. It's my ambition to be selected for the Mind Complex one day!

I've been reading a bit of history about your planet. I found out that Earth has a lot of wars going on. They sound horrible! I am always scared of war because there used to be quite a few on Bartoch. We often learn about them in History class. Like I said, we're very lucky that the Mind Complex has stopped most of them.

I suppose that I told you that my mother originally comes from Tarzak. She had to leave because there was a war with another country on the same island, called Lerzak. It was a very violent time and thousands of people died. My mother often gets sad when we talk about the war. A lot of her family suffered and her youngest brother died in it. I really wish I had met him but he died long before I was born. His name was also Zmod and I'm named after him.

Because my father is in the Bozkinian army my mother sometimes worries about him being sent to a war. But he says that the world is much safer than it used to be. So there is very little chance of that happening now. He says that nowadays the job of the army is to prevent any wars happening. I hope he is right. It still means that he might have to go away for a while.

I've also had a busy week at school. This week for our Protection of the Ground studies class we were allowed to go outside!!! At the moment we are learning about how the poisoned metal called telecterium destroyed our environment. So we went on a field trip to the remains of the Ozul valley. It used to be very beautiful but then it was spoiled in the last century by telecterium. Does it exist on Earth? Here it caused horrible things to happen. It destroyed the ground and killed many living things. But I believe that at first everyone thought this new metal would be very useful, and so they spread it all over the planet. No one can live in these areas now. We all felt very sad walking around there. We were only allowed to stay outside for an hour because the air is too polluted. We were made to wear special protection suits – they were really uncomfortable… I was glad when we were able to go back home. To tell the truth I felt nervous above ground.

Our teacher showed us some pictures of how Bartoch looked three hundred stellar orbits ago. It was amazing, because it was so full of bright colours. Now most of the surface of our planet is orange and disgusting. I really wish we could live like you do on Earth.

Thank you for telling me about football. Actually, it still sounds very strange to me! I cannot imagine playing that on Bartoch. People prefer to play against each other using computers. They can choose from many games, like Eat the Cheat, Volcano Explorer and Control the Jumping Glods. Computers are much better players than Bartochians. I think we would be bored to always play the same game – even if the players change.

Tomorrow I have to take Darak to the vet for a check-up. The vet told me that all glods need to be checked every six months to make sure they are healthy. The vet will probably try to give Darak an injection. Last time we went it was very funny. Let me explain : when the vet tried to give Darak an injection he was sick on him! The vet was really angry. I wanted to laugh but I didn't dare. It was really horrible though because everything was covered with stinking pink slime when we left.

We have a big cave at the back of our house. Darak likes to run around in there. My father built him a small glod hut there. Still Darak prefers to live inside our house. My father was a bit annoyed at first when Darak refused to live in the hut, but now he has got used to it. Sometimes, Darak sleeps in my room because he is scared of the dark. By the way yes, we have plenty of light underground thanks to the Atomic Mirrors. I don't exactly know how they work. I think they get light from above, and then transmit it down here.

I wish you could meet Darak – he is always doing crazy things! Often it gets me into trouble with my parents, especially when he blows his purple pus bubbles all around the place. When they touch something sharp they burst. He only does that when he is happy though. The neighbours get very annoyed with him because he screeches and scratches all night when the moons appear. It is a strange glod habit that no one really understands. I don't care though, because he is so much fun to be with! He always makes me laugh and tries to cheer me up when I am sad!

One time when my mother was baking rooley cakes, Darak went in there and blew really huge pus bubbles on them. My mother was furious and threw things at him, because she had invited guests for that evening and had made lots to eat. After that she became very strict with him and he doesn't dare go into the kitchen now.

Anyway, Darak and I are going out now to hunt for some more rocks. I can see from the way he is scratching that he thinks that we will find some more moving ones. I never used to be able to find moving rocks, but now my collection is suddenly growing!

You've got to tell me all about what you have been doing.

May peace be granted to you! Clotpid huy pek !
Zmod

"That was a great film," said Sirah. "What did you think?"

"I liked the scenes with the operations. They were really horrible!" replied Darius.

"Oh come on," his sister said. "How could you like those - they didn't even look real. I was laughing when they operated on that alien. It looked so fake. I could have done a more convincing job in making the aliens look real."

"Do you think that there are aliens out there?"

"Well you should know – you're writing to one."

"He's not like that! I mean those really strange aliens - the ones that they talk about in the film."

"Well I don't know. Lots of people claim to have been kidnapped."

"Cool!"

Location: London, England
Planet: Earth
Date: 16th April 2286

Dear Zmod

Thank you for your long spacemail.

I really learned so much about Bartoch from your message – your system for controlling the planet is very different to ours! If it stops problems on the planet, then maybe we should have something similar to the Mind Complex! I have to admit though that for us on Earth it sounds like a very weird system. Does it hurt when they take out your brain?

Your stories about Darak were really funny - I laughed a lot when I heard about what happened when you took Darak to the vet. I am surprised that the vet allows him in the surgery now. We often take Ranger to the vet for check-ups. Fortunately, Ranger hasn't done anything bad to our vet like Darak!

On Saturday my sister Sirah took me to the cinema to see a film called *Answers*. It was a strange story about people living in a small town, who believed that they had been kidnapped by aliens from another planet who would perform horrible medical experiments on them. In the final scene, there is a general who explains that aliens had not been kidnapping people. In fact it was the military who wanted to search for the aliens who had escaped from a lost spacecraft that the army had shot down several years earlier. A special unit of the army was kidnapping people and experimenting on them to see if they had any link with the aliens. The aliens were either still alive or had mixed with the local population. Weird!

I thought that it was a very exciting film, but it was also quite scary. There were many disgusting scenes – but I loved them! It was cool when they showed the operations. Sirah thought that the film was strange but she said that in the last century there were often stories about aliens kidnapping people. I suppose that it was because people did not know as much as we do now. Now we know that there are many planets in the universe and we can communicate with them. It's funny to think that people used to believe that aliens wanted to kidnap them! Did Bartochians also believe that in the past?

I don't usually watch the news – it's boring - but this week has been very interesting! On our planet there are many rumours that monsters that were thought to have died hundreds of years ago still exist in underground caves. In one country called Scotland, which is not far from here, an expedition was launched to find a monster that is believed to live in a lake. I've heard lots of stories before about this monster but no one has ever found it. I didn't really pay much attention to this news, but today the explorers said that they had discovered several new caves under the lake. So there's a possibility that something is living there!

Please write and tell me what you have been up to. I always enjoy reading your spacemails.

Your friend
Darius

The International Chronicle

15th March 2286

Will Nessie the monster be found?

By Bob Buscada

The mystery of the Loch Ness Monster, nicknamed "Nessie", has intrigued people for several hundred years, but no one has yet uncovered the truth. Yet, this could all change thanks to the efforts of the African sugar billionaire Morenike Retta. Mr. Retta is travelling to Scotland where he is putting together an international team to explore the Loch.

"I have read about the monster since I was a child," remarked Mr. Retta. "It has always fascinated me and I am determined to find it."

Others who have failed in previous attempts to find the monster are sceptical.

"I can't see how he will succeed," said Colonel Reginald Twistleton-Thomas of the organisation Global Monsterwatch. "He has no experience in this field. We conducted a detailed search of the Loch three years ago using the most modern equipment available and we didn't find a thing."

However, many of the locals are looking forward to the arrival of Mr. Retta.

"I'm delighted that he's launching this expedition," said Hamish McDougal, owner of the Nessie Gift Shop. "It's going to bring hundreds of more tourists to the region - I've already doubled my order for Nessie T-shirts just in case!"

The Vakpak Monitor

19th Harcifion, Hexile 14783

Maverick scientist predicts Jellibech volcano catastrophe

There was fierce debate today at the Annual Planetary Vulcanology Congress (PVC) when maverick scientist, Dr. Coree Mundu, warned that Bozkinians should closely monitor the area around Jellibech Springs. He urged delegates to support him in setting up a taskforce to star work immediately.

"I fear that we are becoming too complacent regarding Jellibech Springs, " said Dr Mundu. "The area around the Springs has become so built up in recent stellar orbits, that if the Arqiat Crater were to erupt, we would face a disaster that we would be ill prepared to deal with. I appeal to my colleagues and the Mind Complex to listen to my reasoning."

This is not the first time that Dr Mundu has courted controversy. Two stellar orbits ago he predicted that the Iluminif volcano on Fernuk was about to erupt and blamed it on outsiders - only for nothing to happen. The warning, which became popularly known as the "Fernukian fiasco", caused severe damage to the tourist industry as hundreds of travellers avoided the area for their holidays. His intervention caused outrage amongst the Fernukians, who accused him of seeking publicity to further his own career.

> Therefore, it comes as little surprise that his latest prediction has been ignored by the Mind Complex and has been flatly rejected by mainstream Bartochian vulcanologists. Their irritation at Dr Mundu's comments were highlighted in a statement by the Chairman of the PVC, Professor Hrzhni Daflink. "The last time that the Arqiat Crater erupted was over a thousand hexicycles ago. Since then it has shown no signs whatsoever of any unusual activity. We are all in agreement that there is no cause for alarm." Professor Daflink's verdict will come as a relief to the Bozkinians. With the tourist season at its highpoint, the last thing they would like to see is a repeat of the Fernukian fiasco.

Location: Vakpak, Bozkin
Planet: Bartoch
Date: 7th Armiun, Hexile 14784

Dear Darius

Thanks for your spacemail.

The film you went to see sounded very interesting, but a bit too scary for me! Yes, we also had many stories on Bartoch in the past that aliens were kidnapping people. Some of them are really stupid stories. I don't like them because they make me feel nervous. There's one really famous story that states that we are not the original inhabitants of Bartoch! According to this, the original population were kidnapped and replaced by us. I hope that's not true.

Actually, the film you saw reminded me of a famous Tarzakian author called Bizio Markif. He lived about 350 stellar orbits ago. He claimed that he had been taken to a different planet by aliens. According to the legend, he was an illiterate farmer before he was taken. He disappeared for ten stellar orbits, but when he came back he was much more intelligent than before and although he looked the same, no one could believe that it was the same person! Many people were scared of him - they chased him out of the city where he lived. Even his family didn't want anything to do with him! Eventually, he was allowed to live on a small island off the coast of the country Fernuk. There he wrote a book called *Beyond the Clouds*. According to him, there was life on other planets and he had seen it. Some of the civilisations on these other planets were very advanced and had spaceships that could fly around the universe. Occasionally, they would visit Bartoch. Strange isn't it ?

One of the interesting things about his book is that we do not know much about him or which planets he actually went to. Who knows – he may have even visited Earth!

Our Experience Books teacher, Mrs. Tigli, studied Bizio Markif's life in detail at university and she told us that he definitely existed. She has even visited his house on the small island off Fernuk. Mrs. Tigli believes that not only did he exist, but that it was impossible for him to have made up his stories. Many of the ideas in his book were too advanced for his time. For example, in his book there is a picture of a machine for flying that looks exactly like a hover jet. We know that four hundred stellar orbits ago people could not fly. How he drew that we don't know.

I suppose that people on all planets have stories about aliens - they had no way of explaining the universe before. If something strange happened, such as the arrival of a comet or a meteor shower, then they blamed it on aliens. It must be worrying not to know what causes these events.

I know that even ten stellar orbits before contact was officially announced between our planets, some Bartochians – "Isolationists" I believe - had picked up communications from outer space. They did not want contact with other planets. So they spread lots of rumours about alien invasions. That made it much harder to tell people about your planet. Even when the first politicians from Earth visited Bartoch in Decile 14566 , they organised violent demonstrations in many cities against them. Fortunately, the Mind Complex manages to control them. Oh I forgot to explain, they don't actually "take away" your brain in there. The brain energy just get mixed with all the other ones!

The Isolationists still exist, but people listen to them less nowadays. Most Bartochians hate them because they place telecterium bombs to kill us. They scare me and so I am glad that the army is always searching for them. Fortunately, most of us want contact with other planets. I don't understand why some people are afraid of different things.

I guess that it is why I enjoy writing to you and

receiving you spacemails - this way we can learn more about life on each other's planets! I am sure that when we eventually meet, it will seem as if we have always known each other!

I had a hard time taking Darak to the vet. It's always a bit difficult because they don't like each other. Darak is so bad. He kept pretending to vomit just to scare the vet. Anyway the vet got his revenge because he gave Darak an injection!

Last week we were lucky again and found more moving rocks. I'm really excited that my collection is growing! Anyway, one of the moving rocks was bright green and I don't know why but Darak really loves this particular green rock! He's been dragging it all around our house and it makes my mother angry because it leaves dust everywhere and scratches the floor. I tried to take the rock from him but he won't let me have it. At the moment he's even sleeping with this rock next to him. Glods are so strange!

By the way, do you have any news about this mysterious monster? We don't have any left on our planet since the Great Telecterium Disaster. It's a pity!

Well, I'm going to have to finish my spacemail now. I have to go and rehearse for the school play.

May peace be granted to you! Clotpid huy pek !
Zmod

Zmod began to walk quickly as he passed the school gates and into the main tunnel walkway. He did not want to run otherwise one of the teachers would probably complain. Last month he had been caught running through the school tunnels by Mr. Dingu, who had placed him in detention for a week. Zmod looked around, but Mr. Dingu was not at his usual place outside the gates. Zmod grinned and started to run.

Suddenly he felt himself lose his balance. Was it his imagination or was the ground shaking? He looked around him. No one else seemed to have noticed – they all seemed to be carrying on with their activities.

He was approaching Jellibech Springs now. He always loved walking through this area because it was so beautiful. There was something strange about it today though. The air had a pungent odour and he was sure that he could see greyish fumes emanating from a hole in the tunnel. He walked to the edge of the path to take a closer look. He picked up a rock and looked at it. It was moving, but why was it such a strange colour? It was not the usual kind of rock in Jellibech Springs. Where had it come from?

"Keep to the main path young man!" It was one of the park rangers.

"Sorry," said Zmod. "I thought that I saw some fumes."

The park ranger laughed. "If you did you'll be the first Bartochian in 80 generations to do so."

Today's journey felt strange, but Zmod could not work out why. He soon forgot though as he rushed to get home with another moving rock for his collection.

Location: London, England
Planet: Earth
Date: 1st August 2286

Dear Zmod

Thank you for your spacemail.

It was interesting to hear about the reaction of people on Bartoch when relations with Earth were first established in 2109 because we have had the same problems. We also have an Isolationist movement on Earth that want to stop us having contact with other planets. They are completely crazy!

I suppose that's why Bizio Markif's book sounded so fascinating. Can you send me one of his stories ? I would love to read about his unusual life. It would be really interesting to know if he visited Earth and if so, what he thought of us! I love reading about mysteries like this!

It was really good when Sirah was home last week from university but as usual we ended up arguing a lot so maybe it's better that she's gone back! When she's here she uses her old room that is next to mine. Often she plays horrible music very loudly. When she is playing something that I don't like, I have to hit the wall until she stops. Then she goes and complains to my mother or father. Typical!

Did I tell you that about six months ago, Sirah

started taking singing and acting lessons? Even though she is studying Cosmic Architecture at university, her ambition is to be a classical musician or a theatre actress! Pathetic really! I know that you like acting but I hate all that stuff – it's boring. My mother takes Sirah every weekend to her singing and drama classes at the Roldi Academy for the Performing Arts. She'll have to take lots of extra exams in her holidays. She told me that as well as learning how to sing, she has to learn the theory of music. So she will be able to write her own songs. Sometimes she practices her compositions in her room and I make fun of her. Her singing is so bad that it sounds like Ranger barking! I think that Ranger and her could form a group. He would be the talented one!

I suppose I told you that my father is a pilot? Anyway, he usually flies routes to countries that are only a few hours away, but from next week, he will be flying to New China, which is a small country on the opposite side of the planet. It is made of three tiny islands. Actually, there used to be a much bigger island near there but it was destroyed by an asteroid, so it's quite exciting for us that he is going to this part of the planet – my mother seems worried though! I will miss him not being around in the evenings during the week, but he'll only be gone for two months.

It's strange because there is a big time difference between New China and us – I think that it is around 14 atomic revolutions! That means that when I am getting up in the morning, it is already evening there! Then when it is late at night here, it is around lunchtime on the following day for them! Isn't that weird? It means that it is going to be hard for my father to stay in contact with us during the week. My mother has already told him that he better not make a mistake with the time difference when he calls. If he calls early in the morning by mistake she will be really annoyed!

Hey, unfortunately I haven't heard anything interesting about the Nessie monster. Either they're still looking for it or the whole thing was a joke.

Right, I have to go and get ready now. My mother is saying that we must go shopping straight after lunch. I am dreading this afternoon!

Please spacemail me soon. Good luck with getting that green rock away from Darak!

Your friend
Darius

Bizio: Your Majesty, I am afraid that we must flee the city. The volcano looks like it will erupt at any moment.

Queen Jingli: Calm down Councillor. The elders say that it is nothing more than a minor incident. I am sure that no harm will come to us.

Bizio: I am sorry your Majesty, but I feel that we are being complacent.

Queen Jingli: Why do you insist on panicking?

The volcano has behaved in this way on several other occasions.

Bizio: Your Majesty, I feel very strongly that this time it is different. There have been rumblings from the volcano for three days now. That is far too long. Let us evacuate people just in case.

Queen Jingli (suddenly growing angry): Councillor, you are in no position to issue orders to your Queen. If you and your friends wish to flee then so be it. You are dismissed from my service.

Bizio reluctantly withdraws from the chamber and joins his companions. They enter the secret tunnel that will take them out of the city to safety.

The noises outside are growing louder and the sky begins to turn black, but Queen Jingli remains in her chamber.

Queen Jingli (turns to the audience): I do not fear the future for I know that we will be saved. Only those that hold firm to their beliefs can avoid disaster.

The curtain falls.

The audience got to their feet and began to clap and cheer loudly. Zmod's mother and father were the first to do so. They were so proud that Zmod had acted so well!

Location: Vakpak, Bozkin
Planet: Bartoch
Date: 61st Armiun, Hexile 14784

Dear Darius

Thank you for your message. I've decided to answer your spacemail now because I'm not allowed to go to school. I have to stay at home. When it rains we have to stay inside because otherwise we might get covered in dangerous pollutants from the sky. They come through the rocks with the rain. It's depressing to stay inside all day – I hate it! I hope it doesn't rain tomorrow as well. Darak is getting annoyed because we can't go rock hunting.

Next week the tourist season will start and lots of people will start visiting Bozkin. Many of them will want to visit Jellibech Springs, so it makes it difficult for us to go to school. They make the tunnels so crowded! Many of the tourists believe that if they touch the pools of neon they will get younger. The park rangers try to stop them because the neon is very hot and they often forget to wait until it cools.

When they visit the Arqiat Crater, the tourists are supposed to follow a special path. It has small barriers around it. The problem is that many tourists want to get better photos. So they often climb over the barriers! I think that they are totally mad because the inside of the volcano is very steep and at the bottom it is boiling hot. A few stellar orbits ago one tourist did fall into the volcano and so they brought in stricter rules for the tourists. That's why I'm surprised that people are ignoring them again.

Did I tell you that we are going on holiday next week to Tarzak? We will only be there for a week, but I can't wait! It will be good to get outside. We often go to stay with my aunt – she is my mother's sister. I like visiting my cousins. They are great fun and I never get bored when I am with them. My father has said that he will show me more of the Tarzakian countryside this time. He said that since my mother is from there I should at least learn something about the country. I know he is right but when it's a case of going into the hills with my cousins or going to visit a big museum I know which I would prefer to do!

I know you don't like acting but my play went very well. I think that you would have enjoyed it. The only bad part was that Darak wasn't allowed in. He would have caused too much noise anyway and would have probably tried to join in! He is in a happy mood at the moment because he is coming with us to Tarzak. I really don't know how he understands these things!

By the way, I'm sending you a small chapter from Bizio Markif's book *Beyond the Clouds*. The book itself is a bit long - it actually comes in seventeen electro-scrolls. Maybe you won't want to read all of it? I don't know if you will like it though because it is a little strange. He wrote in a very bizarre way. We have to study it for school and so we are not always keen to read it! This chapter I am sending you is the first one and it is about his meeting with the aliens whose spaceship crashed on his farm and who took him to their planet. Let me know what you think of it.

I'm a bit disappointed that there is no news about the monster. It sounded very exciting!

I will try and send you a spacemail from Tarzak!

May peace be granted to you! Clotpid huy pek!
Zmod

Prologue:

As I start this journal dear Reader, I do not know whether to be hopeful or to be sad.

My sadness comes from knowing that there has been no one during my lifetime, who has considered that I might be telling the truth about the marvellous events I witnessed when I was spirited away from this world all those long months ago. On the other hand, I am hopeful that some day there will be those with minds open enough to understand that what we see and behold on our planet does not represent the limits of what occurs in nature. Far beyond the clouds that mark the boundaries of our planet, lie wondrous places with a rich tapestry of life that I have had the good fortune to experience. There lie realms where your troubles simply disappear, where life occurs for the pleasure of living.

My story is long and I struggle to put into words what I have seen and experienced. Perhaps the best

39

way is to relate the events from that fateful day that changed my life forever. It was a day that transformed me from an illiterate farmer into an educated scholar and yet it also changed me from an accepted member of my community into a social outcast. But if the price of social exclusion means that I have been the first one from my planet to witness the true wondrous nature of our universe, then it is a sacrifice I wholly accept.

Therefore, it is to you my dear Readers of the future that I leave these documents.

Chapter One

It was during the mid-stellar orbit harvest season that they arrived. I remember it well because the zin zin plants had produced the best yield for many stellar orbits. All the farmers were happy that they would at last be able to provide for their families after the many stellar orbits of famine. I was on my own, after my wife and daughter's death during the Great Famine, and I was still struggling to feed myself. At last I saw a way out of the cycle of misery and I felt renewed optimism about my life.

I was in the field, at the back of my farmhouse, gathering stalks to place into bundles. Cutting down the stalks was hard work and I was sweating under the mid day sun. The white casing of the plants reflected the sun's rays and my eyes struggled to focus against the glare.

Suddenly I felt the glare lessen. I looked up at the clouds and they seemed to darken. I put down my knife and watched as a large grey object slowly emerged from the sky above me. It seemed to hang there for a moment and then its descent quickened. As it got closer, a shadow began to spill over the field. I realised that the object was about to crash and so I started to run. Yet there was nothing I could do to escape its course and I watched the object pass just over my head and crash into the side of the farmhouse.

I must have passed out because the next thing I remember was waking up in the barn. I had a burning sensation in my head. I had not been able to outrun the object and so I knew that someone had brought me there. I looked up and grew fearful, as my gaze was met by a large, oval, grey face dominated by two large black eyes. Whatever this creature was, it was not from our planet and I began to panic.

The strange alien being sensed my fear and began to communicate with me. It did not speak, but seemed able to transmit its message directly to my mind. It told me that it did not want to harm me and that it wanted to communicate with me. I tried to sit up, but the burning sensation in my head made me dizzy. The alien sensed my pain and placed its hand in front of my face. All at once my pain was gone.

When I was able to stand up, I noticed that we were not alone. Several other grey aliens began to appear from behind the pillars of the barn. I sensed a kind of shyness on their part and it put me at ease. I felt confident and I signalled to them that they were welcome in my home. The aliens sensed my thoughts and suddenly I could feel them communicating excitedly with each other. They too seemed reassured. The first alien turned to me and let me know that he needed my help.

They called themselves the Visitors. They had spent generations travelling through the universe and our planet was simply one place of rest out of numerous other locations. The claimed to have been to our planet before, but it was many centuries before my birth. They had been visiting our planet again as part of a small group, but their spacecraft had become separated. It had malfunctioned and so they needed to await help from their colleagues. I sensed that they were nervous about being on our planet and so I asked why. They told me that during their last visit to a foreign planet, some of the native people had captured one of their group and had killed him. The killing of one of their kind seemed to greatly shock them. I could sense their anxiety as they related the story to me. Therefore, they were very keen to regroup with their colleagues.

I assured them that they would be safe in my house and that they could stay until their colleagues arrived. As there were so many of them I decided that it would be best to let them stay in the barn. However, the first thing I wanted to do was to hide any evidence of their landing. Upon closer inspection, their craft was much smaller than I had initially thought. It was a silver cylindrical object with wing-like projections over its smooth surface. On the underside there lay the entrance to the vessel, which was covered with a translucent hatch. It was just about possible to visualise the outline of various structures inside. The underside of the vessel was charred and the metal appeared to have buckled around the entrance hatch.

Their leader started to tell me about their voyage. He told me that their home lay a great distance away and that the journey required great preparation. They had set off with three other vessels, but they had lost contact with them as they descended through the clouds on our planet. He told me that they had encountered a great mountain surrounded by flames and black smoke. I recognised this to be the Arina volcano. Arina was well known for its occasional eruptions, which would disrupt the weather for miles around. Some said that the famines that we had experienced in recent stellar orbits were due to the great eruption of Arina that took place seven seasons ago.

From what they told me, their vessel had passed directly above the mountain and their flight path had been disrupted. They must have been travelling at a tremendous speed for the Arina volcano lay at least three days journey from the village. Whoever these aliens were, their technology was far more advanced than anything we could even dream of.

As I spent more time with them, I began to feel comfortable being around them. Although they were more advanced than us, I did not feel threatened by them. They questioned me endlessly about matters that appeared trivial. They wanted to know about different situations I had experienced in my life and how I had dealt with them. Ordinary emotions, such as happiness or sadness seemed to fascinate them and to intrigue them. They did not appear to experience the same extremes of emotions as we were capable of. Perhaps we had something that they lacked and so wished to learn from. However, at this point I did not know what that was.

Just as the sun was rising, I heard a low rumbling sound. It appeared to be some way off and to I went out into the field to investigate. For a time I could only hear the sound, but then a silver cylindrical vessel began to descend from the sky. I knew at once that these were the colleagues of the aliens. I returned into the barn to tell them, but somehow they already knew that their rescuers were on the way. No doubt they had been in contact with each other as their arrival became imminent. The aliens rushed around the barn, preparing themselves for the arrival of their colleagues.

The rumbling noise became louder and the spacecraft's descent began to shake the structure of the barn. I began to fear that the beams of the barn would give way, but they were sturdier than I realised and only buckled slightly. Once the craft had landed, I noticed that a hatch opened on the side of the vessel and that a ramp emerged. The vessel was far bigger than the one that the aliens had arrived in, which explained the noise as it landed.

The aliens began to run towards the ramp. The leader of the alien group turned to me and simply asked, "Come with us." It was a strange request and yet it in an unusual way it seemed to make sense.

These aliens intrigued me and an overwhelming desire to learn more about them overcame me. If I stayed in my home, life would plod along in its usual way. I would no doubt be struggling for survival with all the other farmers. I was under no illusion that the recent good zin zin yield was temporary. I was sure that we would enter a period of famine the next stellar orbit, which is why I had worked so hard to exploit the benefits of this stellar orbit's harvest.

Here was an opportunity to discover something new – something that an ordinary person such as myself would never normally get a chance to experience.

I told the alien that I accepted his offer and I began to follow him up the ramp to the vessel. Little did I know how much this decision would change my life. As the door closed, I took one final look at my home and knew that I had no regrets.

Darius hated shopping in the centre of London. There were too many people. Since he had argued with his mother so much inside the shop she had told him to wait outside until she had finished. He was sure that she would take a long time so he decided to explore the street a bit. There was a lot to see and he had plenty of time.

"Hey kid, take our photo." Darius took the digital electrocube from the burly tourist and began to focus on the couple. "Hurry up will you", yelled the tourist. "I don't want to die of old age."

Darius frowned and then very deliberately focused the electrocube on a fence to the right of the couple. "Smile please," he asked them politely.

The tourist grabbed the electrocube roughly from Darius' hand. Darius walked off and laughed. If they bothered to look those stupid tourists were in for a shock.

Faiz Kermani

Location: London, England
Planet: Earth
Date: 9th October 2286

Dear Zmod

Thank you for your spacemail.

Bizio Markif's story was fantastic! I'd love to have done what he did. Travelling with aliens like that would be great! I would be able to get away from school and learn things that are really interesting!

There were lots of tourists when I went shopping with my mother! I hate them! They make the city even more crowded. Also, since they don't know how to get around the city they often stand in the way of everyone else and block the streets!

There are many places in London that the tourists like to visit. I think most of them are boring and I don't understand why they get so excited to visit them. If you are unlucky to be near these places you can hardly move. One of the most popular places is Buckingham Palace where the President lives. Around 2100, England used to have a Royal family and the King lived in the palace. The Royal family became very unpopular because they kept wasting public money. The last King didn't have any children and so the Royal Family tried to pretend that one of his friend's sons was actually his! Unfortunately for him, when this man was about to become King someone found out the secret. The ordinary people got very angry and because they were so fed up they kicked the Royal Family out.

My great-grandfather says that when he was young

48

he never believed that the monarchy would end. He says that the ancestors of the last King took power over a thousand years ago and so people had become used to having a Royal family. For me it's weird to think we used to have a monarchy in this country! Yet for people like my great-grandfather it is very strange that they don't exist now!

Anyway, I've got to go and start working on an essay for my Diplomacy class. I've decided to write one about how we could have avoided the Great Canine Death - it needs to be finished by next week.

By the way don't worry about the monster story. If I hear anything about it I'll let you know!

I am looking forward to your spacemail from Tarzak!

Your friend
Darius

Location: Nihotepec, Tarzak
Planet: Bartoch
Date: 71st Armiun, Hexile 14784

Dear Darius

Hello from Tarzak!!! We arrived here a few days ago and we are staying with my aunt and uncle and cousins. My aunt Douria, is the younger sister of my mother.

I am really happy to be here. As I'm an only child, I always like visiting my cousins because they are such fun. I have two cousins, Raglu and Glacq, they are both boys, and my uncle is called Trebit. He is a glacier engineer and he is very serious. He is a bit grumpy and can be very strict - when he is around, I behave myself because otherwise he shouts at me. Darak is very scared of him and tries to avoid him. My father gets on better with him than the rest of us - I am very glad that he is here otherwise Uncle Trebit always checks on me to see what I'm doing.

Raglu has got his flying licence and has a small hydro skimmer. So on the day we arrived, he decided to take me, his brother Glacq and Darak into the hills for the day. I think it was also to get away from Uncle Trebit because he started to complain that we were making too much noise.

Glacq also has a glod, called Pulvi and he came along with us. It is good that Pulvi was there because otherwise Darak gets very bored. Sometimes he bounces around so much that we don't have the energy to chase after him. He never stops! Pulvi is the same so at least they could keep each other company.

I love Tarzak because we can go outside – it is almost impossible to do that in Bozkin. In Tarzak you can see the sky very clearly. You can even see the horizon – really amazing! I like sleeping outside at night and watching the moonrises.

Yesterday my father arrived in Tarzak. He was supposed to come with us but he got delayed because of his work. He was annoyed because they made him take part in an emergency rescue exercise. The army have to do this every few stellar orbits because of the Isolationists. The Mind Complex always makes sure that it is a surprise so that they are ready for any situation.

Anyway, now that my father is here, he is very keen to show me some of the history of Tarzak. He was here during the Civil War as part of the peacekeeping force. I wanted to see where he had served.

The first place he took me to was the border with Lerzak. The border is also known as the Grey Line as it was the furthest that the Lerzakian troops reached during the Civil War. The Grey Line a very strange place to be, because although there is no violence you can feel the tension. I was a bit scared.

Lerzak is ruled by a dictator called General Aghar – he is really mad and dangerous. He wanted to conquer Tarzak and so in the past he launched a surprise invasion. Luckily, the Tarzakian army put up a lot of resistance – far more than he expected!

Eventually the Mind Complex got involved. At first General Aghar tried to ignore them. But they are so powerful he had to obey. Thanks to them there has been peace for several stellar orbits. I hope that one day they will get rid of General Aghar though, because he is so nasty. He scares me.

After we visited the Grey Line, we visited the war cemetery in west Tarzak. There is a statue there of my uncle Zmod. I probably told you that I am named after him. I am very proud to be related to him as he is so famous on Tarzak. When people on Tarzak find out that

I am his nephew they get very excited! For my mother the trip to the cemetery is not a happy one. She cries a lot, as Zmod was her brother. Whenever we come to Tarzak, we try to visit the war cemetery so that we can pay our respects. In Tarzakian culture it is the custom to visit the cemetery at sunset. This is when we feel closest to our ancestors. Another thing we do is to throw three small stones over our heads, which shows that we have not forgotten the past – even though it is behind us.

Well I'm going to end my spacemail now because I am being called for dinner. If I don't go soon, Uncle Trebit will come looking for me.

I hope you enjoyed hearing about Tarzak. Please write soon and tell me what you have been doing.

May peace be granted to you! Clotpid huy pek!
Zmod

68th Armiun,
Hexile 14784

Tonight Dounipian Broadcasting Corporation is pleased to bring you an exclusive interview with General Aghar, Chief Councillor of Lerzak. Our award-winning reporter, Tchizia Garnish, is the first foreign reporter to have ever been granted such an interview.

Garnish: General, if I may, I would like to start by asking you about Bartoch's relations with other planets. You have never really been in favour of external contact have you?

General Aghar: We believe that societies on Bartoch would progress more if contact with other planets were stopped. It is outside influences that are responsible for many of the problems we are now facing, such as pollution and corruption.

Garnish: Will you be accepting the decision of the Mind Complex regarding the banning of the Isolationists? Some people believe that you support their attacks.

General Aghar: That is not true. We have no connection with the Isolationist movement. We believe that a peaceful solution to the problem is the only way forward and so we support the decision of the Mind Complex.

Zmod switched off the television in disgust. What a liar! The way that General Aghar spoke, he almost sounded like a reasonable person. A stranger watching that interview would never have guessed that this very same man was responsible for millions of deaths of innocent Bartochians.

Location: London, England
Planet: Earth
Date: 34th November 2286

Dear Zmod

Thank you for your message from Tarzak. Sorry that I have taken a while to reply.

I was very interested to hear about Tarzak's history. I'm glad that the Mind Complex were able to stop the war. We really need a system like that on our planet!

Our school term ends in a week. I am looking forward to that because then we will have holidays for one month. My father told me that when he was a child their summer holidays lasted nearly three months! I wish we still had that system!

Did I tell you about our football competition? It was a disaster! We had been hoping to reach the final of the local competition for the first time, but we were beaten 401-0. I was angry because the team we made an alliance with at the beginning suddenly attacked us half way through the game – we shouldn't have trusted them! That is the heaviest defeat we have ever experienced. It was very embarrassing because all our families were there watching us.

I felt angry afterwards on the way home. My mother and father said that I shouldn't be upset because we had done well to reach the semi-final, but I still felt terrible. Sirah told me that we were lucky – at least it hadn't been 501-0. I didn't really appreciate her joke! It's annoying because it is the end of the football season for us. We won't have a chance for revenge until next season.

Well I'm going to end this spacemail now because I've been asked to clean my room by my parents. I hate doing that but I've been able to avoid it for a week because I said that I was busy with my schoolwork. Now that it is finished I have no escape!

Please spacemail again soon.

Your friend
Darius

A Short History of The Mind Complex

- by Arindy Joluba, Candidate Elect

'A merging of the best minds on the planet in order to prevent self-inflicted destruction' was how the Fernukian philosopher Idiri Maloon first described the concept of the Mind Complex in his treatise No Return to the Past. Yet despite the book becoming a Bartochian philosophy classic, the concepts explored by Maloon remained as academic theories for a number of stellar orbits.

'Maloon's ideas were too advanced for their time,' states his official biographer, Professor Voralee Dolkin. 'Sadly it took the devastation of the Second Thermonuclear War for us to wake up and realise that we could no longer go on running our planet based on a country by country governmental basis.'

Following the signing of the peace treaty between the three Provincial Powers, it was agreed that a new system for controlling events on the planet would be set up that would eliminate bias to any one country. Two stellar orbits later, delegates from the three Provincial Powers agreed to form the Mind Complex and put forward suitable candidates to be judged for inclusion on the basis of Maloon's Seven Criteria of Objectivity. In their now famous declaration of Chuplix it was declared that 'the major challenge for the Mind Complex will be to begin the transition of our planet from a culture of war and destruction to a culture of freedom, tolerance and communication.'

Location: Vakpak, Bozkin
Planet: Bartoch
Date: 3rd Sentinum, Hexile 14784

Dear Darius

Thank you for your spacemail. I was sorry to hear that you lost in your football match. Maybe you will do better next time!

I am back at home now. We got delayed on our way back from Tarzak because one of the main tunnel routes was blocked by falling rocks. No one really knows what happened. We had to stay in the tunnel for five hours before we could get home. Some people think that Isolationists might have been trying to blow up the tunnel. Other people are scared that the volcano might be active again. My father said it was just a coincidence. He says that tunnels often get blocked like this. That's why I hate living underground – it never feels really safe.

My grandfather has come to stay with us for a few days before going to his home in Goplin, which is in the north of Bozkin. Tomorrow he has invited all of us to lunch at Bodloo's restaurant in central Vakpak. Bodloo's restaurant is very well known in Vakpak, so it is going to be very exciting! On their menu they say that you can order any type of food on the planet. Sometimes people try to order very strange things from other parts of Bartoch just to see if this is true. One of them is called East pole rock soup – it really has rock dust in it! I think it tastes horrible, but many Bartochians say that it is good for digestion. Another one that I think is strange is called Robingo sea cutlet, which comes from Fernuk. It is made from a mixture of special deep-sea creatures and it changes colour whilst you eat it!

I like it when my grandfather takes us there because he actually knows the Bodloo family. Fligon Bodloo, who is the son of the owner, was one of his students at Goplin university. He used to teach Geology there. My mother jokes that everyone on the planet was a student of my grandfather at one point in their lives. He seems to know so many people! It's good that he knows the Bodloo family because I'm sure we will get a very nice table in the restaurant. A lot of famous people go to Bodloo's restaurant, so I'm very excited! I've been allowed to take Darak with me so I hope he'll behave! I'm a bit worried that he might try to steal food from other people in the restaurant. He will eat anything!

Well I had better finish this spacemail because my mother wants me to sleep earlier tonight. Even though I don't have school tomorrow she won't let me stay up late. She says that it is not good to get into the habit of staying up too late and that I must still be tired after the journey back from Tarzak.

May peace be granted to you! Clotpid huy pek!
Zmod

"Has it been confirmed as an incident then?"

Zmod heard his father speaking very quietly to someone. He didn't look happy at all.

"OK, I'll be there."

His father caught sight of him as he closed the main door.

"Go back to sleep Zmod."

"Is it about the tunnel accident?"

"No, no. It isn't. It's something different – but they want me at the base. Go back to your room."

Zmod didn't know what was going on, but something wasn't right. They never called his father out like this. How could he sleep when he was scared?

12th December 2286

And now live from Loch Ness, Lothian television brings you an interview with Mr. Morenike Retta, who has agreed to speak to our reporter Helena Wills.

Helena Wills: Mr. Retta, you must be delighted with the progress so far. How big are these new caves that you have found under the lake?

Morenike Retta: Yes, Helena. It's been great so far! We're not sure exactly how big these caves are, but our tests suggest that they could run for miles underground. Our submarines were able to enter some of these caves so we have pretty good information on them.

Helena Wills: Is there any chance that monsters are living down there?

Morenike Retta: It's a little early to be sure, but we've found what looks like footprints at one of the entrances to the caves. The caves would certainly be big enough to support life of this sort. In a few of them we were able to surface and go above ground.

Helena Wills: When do you think we'll know?

Morenike Retta: Our scientists are analysing the information we have collected now. If they think that a particular cave is worth us investigating we'll send a team back there by the end of the week.

Location: London, England
Planet: Earth
Date: 15th January 2287

Dear Zmod

Thank you for your spacemail. Happy New Year! I can't believe that it is already one year since we have been writing to each other!

Now we also have school holidays for two weeks. It's great to be able to get up late, but I miss my friends. Unless there is a lot to do I get a bit bored. Anyway, at least it will give me a chance to finish off this spacemail to you. I started it yesterday but because there was some exciting news about that monster expedition I didn't get very far!

By the way, according to the news, the people on that expedition I was talking about think that they might have found a monster!!! At the moment they can't tell us exactly what it looks like, but they've found big footprints near an underground cave. Some people say that the monster will look like a dinosaur, which is a creature that used to live on our planet in ancient times. Some people are saying that the explorers also found a huge wing – this could mean that the monster can fly! The skin on this wing is supposed to glow in the dark! How cool!

I really hope they find the monster and that we get to see it! It's going to be very exciting! Don't worry, I'll keep you up to date on what is happening!

Please spacemail me soon.

Your friend
Darius

Location: Vakpak, Bozkin
Planet: Bartoch
Date: 1st Degrium, Hexile 14784

Dear Darius

Thank you for your spacemail. That's incredible news about the monster! Do you have any more information about it? I've been listening to the news on our planet, but they haven't even mentioned it. I wonder how an ancient monster could have survived for so long?

I'm also really amazed that we have been writing to each other for so long! It is so nice to have a friend on Earth. I know that all my friends are quite envious! I really enjoy it when we learn about Earth in our Astronomy classes because I feel that I already know a lot about it thanks to you. I'm looking forward to learning even more from your spacemails!

I've got to go now because it's late and I have to find Darak. As soon as it gets dark, he likes to go and screech when the moons rise but it makes the neighbours very angry. There are some other glods in these tunnels and when they are all screeching together it is really horrible! I think that they try to compete with each other. They are such strange creatures! Some of our neighbours have said that they will call the authorities to take away the glods if they continue to be noisy at night. I don't want them to take away Darak! He is the loudest and I'm sure they'll try to get him first! Anyway, it is never difficult to find him. At the moment, he takes his favourite bright green rock with him and all I have to do is follow the dust and scratch marks!

I hope you will spacemail me again soon!

May peace be granted to you! Clotpid huy pek!
Zmod

The International Chronicle

20th February 2287

Monster explorer on the road to recovery!

Famous monster investigator, Morenike Retta, is recovering in hospital today after his dramatic rescue from the caves beneath Loch Ness. Doctors will not reveal the full details but he is believed to have suffered gas poisoning.

"Poisonous gases could have been building up in those caves for thousands of years," remarked Malcolm Durwood, Professor of Toxicology at London City Hospital. "The explorers may have just been unfortunate enough to become exposed to them. I doubt that it has anything to do with a monster."

Location: Paris, France
Planet: Earth
Date: 32nd March 2287

Dear Zmod

I hope you get this space-card because I am sending it from a computer in another Earth country called France – it's great! We are here for a few days.

We are visiting Paris, which is the capital city. France is very close to England but there is a sea in between called the English Channel. We came to France in a hydrotrain that travels through a tunnel under the sea. It is a really amazing journey - it only takes fifteen minutes. When this tunnel was built last century I think the journey used to take three hours! In the past the train used to come out of the tunnel near the coast. Now the tunnel runs under the ground all the way from London and right until we reach Paris. It's great because it saves so much time!

In France they speak a different language called Pan-European. I am learning it at school but I don't like it. My mother speaks it fluently because she studied in France when she was younger.

We are staying with some friends of my mother in the centre of the city – it's good because they have been showing us around and they live close to the main sites. Yesterday they took us to the ruins that are at the top of this space-card. The ruins are of a famous building called the Eiffel tower. They say that when it existed it was possible to see the whole of Paris from the top! That would be so great if we could still go up the tower. I could throw things at all the other tourists below!

My father wants to take me and my sister Sirah to a famous museum called the Louvre, but I don't want to go. Museums are boring! When we go with my father he takes a long time to look at everything. I don't understand the point of it. I'm hoping that he will go with Sirah and that I can find an excuse to stay at home!

I'll send you another spacemail when we get back to London - I'm secretly hoping we get delayed on the way back! It might be an excuse to escape my Maths test at school. I hate my Maths lessons – all we seem to have at the moment are tests.

Ardiuh canta – this is Pan-European for good-bye.

Darius

Location: Vakpak, Bozkin
Planet: Bartoch
Date: 58th Degrium, Hexile 14784

Dear Darius

Thanks for your fantastic space-card from France. That tower must have been incredible when it existed! We don't have anything like that on Bartoch. It was

amazing to read about a different country on your planet!

My Astronomic Geography teacher, Mr. Garbur, told me that he had the chance to visit France when he visited your planet. He was actually there at the time of the invasion, just after this big tower was bombed. It is always very interesting to hear his stories about his time on Earth and he loves to talk about it! Often we try to get him to speak about his travels on your planet because then he talks so much that he forgets to collect our homework!

Is there any more news about the search for that monster? You've got to let me know!

Clotpid huy pek!
Zmod

Location: London, England
Planet: Earth
Date: 18th June 2287

Dear Zmod

Thank you for your spacemail. I'm glad that you received my space-card from France. I enjoyed myself a lot there and I'm hoping to go back soon. We were only there for a few days but I think I picked up a lot of the language so hopefully next time I will be able to speak more with our friends there!

The only bad thing about holidays is when they are over! I really didn't want to go back to school when we returned. Worst of all was that when I got back, my first class was Maths. I must have had very bad luck!

Sorry that I didn't tell you about the search for that monster! The news has been very exciting! The explorers did find the monster but it escaped! They saw its long tail and tried to chase it through the caves, but unfortunately for them it decided to defend itself by releasing a smelly gas – I'm sure you can guess from where! The explorers were knocked out by the terrible odour and they had to be rescued. I shouldn't really say so, but it was very funny! They were very embarrassed when they came out of hospital. At first they tried to cover the whole thing but a journalist found out. I couldn't stop laughing because one of the explorers said that he was very angry with the monster and threatened to go back into the cave and kill it for attacking him. However, a lot of people support the monster and say that it should be left alone. It's going to be interesting to see what happens next! I hope it returns!

Well, please write soon!

Your friend
Darius

The International Chronicle

1st April 2287

Explorer denies threat to monster

Discoverer of the Loch Ness monster, Morenike Retta, yesterday denied that one of his team had threatened to kill the creature.

"I know it sounded bad, but he didn't mean what he said," laughed Mr. Retta. "Unfortunately Fred got the full force of the blast when we were in the cave because he was at the front. He was only expressing his frustration at not being able to catch the monster."

Mr. Retta's team has now applied for an official permit to capture the monster and plans to place it in a zoo. However, local people are upset at these plans.

"The monster should be allowed to stay in his home," said Angus MacDonald, chairman of the newly formed Save our Nessie campaign. "We've asked for volunteers to come to the Loch to prevent the explorers going back there to catch him."

Location: Vakpak, Bozkin
Planet: Bartoch
Date: 4th Rhodiun, Hexile 14785

Dear Darius

Thanks for your spacemail. It was interesting to hear what happened to the monster! I suppose that it has a right to defend itself. I hope they don't allow that explorer to go back into the cave.

I've had a terrible week! I broke my arm coming back from school. I probably told you that I hate hospitals so I was quite worried when I had to go there. I was lucky though because a very nice doctor treated me.

I have to go and take Darak to the vet again. He is due to have some vaccinations for ginji fever. It is an illness that is caused by small creatures called ginjis that live in stagnant helium ponds. These ponds often stink a lot, but glods seem to love them! I don't know what I'm going to do... as I told you Darak doesn't like the vet - and the vet doesn't really like him!

The weather has been really strange for the last few weeks, but no one seems to know why. Usually it is cold at this time of the stellar orbit, but the air feels quite warm and so it is hard to sleep at night. Also, the air often smells a bit strange. Darak hates it. At the moment, it is very hard for us to stop him from bouncing around and screeching. It makes me worried when he is like that. He has also been behaving strangely when we go rock hunting. Usually he likes to catch moving rocks but he seems scared of them now. He just won't go near them. When I try to put his favourite moving rock next to him he pushes it away. I can't understand why he is suddenly so afraid.

Maybe it is just because he knows that we are taking him to the vet. He always acts in a strange way when we are thinking of going there. I don't know how he manages to understand these things… But he has no escape from the vet this time!

May peace be granted to you! Clotpid huy pek!
Zmod

Zmod lay in the ambulance groaning in pain.

He couldn't understand how it had happened. He had been walking back through the tunnel from school when he had suddenly lost his balance. He had tried to grab onto the side rail but it seemed to have snapped off and so he fell. His arm hit a large rock and then he passed out.

The paramedics rushed him through to the laser surgery department.

"I'm afraid that your arm is broken young Zmod," said Dr. Jotni.

"How long do you think it will take to heal?" Zmod asked anxiously.

"Oh we can fix it in a few minutes."

Zmod felt nervous as the scanner was activated. Dr.

Jotni passed the scanner over his bed. As he focused the scanner on Zmod's arm, Zmod noticed a screen at the side of his bed. He watched in astonishment as an image of the broken bone appeared. He soon forgot the pain in his arm as he watched the image become clearer. He could see a definite gap between two pieces of bone.

"That break looks serious" he said sadly.

"I'm afraid so," replied Dr. Jotni. "You have had a nasty knock, but like I said we'll soon fix that. How did you do it?"

"I don't really know. I was walking along pretty normally and then I lost my balance and fell."

"Hmm - well you must have been doing something strange to get a big break like this!"

At first, the laser made no noise at all. Zmod wondered if it was having any effect at all. Suddenly he felt a vibrating feeling in his arm. He started to laugh because it tickled.

"Zmod, you must keep still, otherwise the bone won't grow back straight," said Dr. Jotni sternly.

Zmod tried very hard not to laugh, but the tickling feeling was almost unbearable. He stared at the white ceiling. Perhaps if he distracted himself he would be able to stop laughing. It was very difficult and he had to bite his tongue in order to stop himself giggling.

As soon as Dr. Jotni put the laser down, Zmod burst out laughing. It didn't matter now that Dr. Jotni had finished. Slowly the tickling feeling began to disappear from his arm and Zmod stopped giggling.

"Is my arm OK then?"

"Yes – it's as good as new," said Dr. Jotni. "You'll

need to give it a rest for a week, so be very careful. I don't want you having any other strange falls OK?"

Zmod felt embarrassed – it really hadn't been his fault.

Location: London, England
Planet: Earth
Date: 1st August 2287

Dear Zmod

Thank you for your spacemail.

I hope your arm is better now. It sounded like a bad accident, but the doctor must have done an excellent job! Here on Earth, it would be impossible for them to heal a broken bone so quickly! When I broke my leg a few years ago playing football, it took nearly two months to heal properly. I wasn't allowed to play any sports for a long time. It was really annoying.

By the way, a campaign has started to save the Loch Ness monster. One of the explorers has been trying to get permission to go back into the caves but fortunately the government of Scotland refused. The explorer said that he only wants to capture the monster but no one believes him now. Anyway, no one knows where the monster has gone. There hasn't been any sign of it since the explorers were rescued. Maybe the monster was scared and decided to go somewhere else.

This week is going to be very exciting because my parents are planning our end of term holiday. As my father is an airline pilot he can get very cheap tickets for us. If my father can find us tickets for a good price then we will go to Brazil because my mother has some relatives there. I can't wait for that because I have never been to Brazil before! It will be good to get away from school!

Spacemail me soon.

Your friend
Darius

The International Chronicle

11th August 2287

Nessie spotted in Japan!

Following the dramatic escape from explorers in February the Loch Ness Monster has suddenly reappeared at the Hakone Yumoto Onsen hot springs in Japan.

"I was relaxing in the hot water when there was a crashing sound and the monster surfaced near us," exclaimed Japanese eye witness Hideyuki Miyoshi. "At first I thought it was an earthquake. All the buildings started to collapse and people were running from the springs screaming. We were terrified!"

According to witnesses the monster had a thick body, with a long thin neck that led to a small head. The creature was generally grey in colour, but certain people reported that its neck had several round glowing patches. The monster moved in a jerky manner above ground and appeared to move more gracefully when in the water.

The sudden appearance of the monster on the other side of the planet has baffled oceanographers around the world. Its re-emergence could suggest previously undiscovered links between underground caves around the world.

> "There is no way that the monster could have reached Japan by swimming at sea. Someone would have spotted it long ago," remarked monster expert Dr Murray Michael. "It's going to make it very difficult for us to catch as it looks as if it can disappear into underground tunnels and reappear anywhere on the planet."

Location: London, England
Planet: Earth
Date: 23rd October 2287

Dear Zmod

How are you? I haven't heard from you for quite a few months. I hope everything is OK.

Our school holidays have started so I am really happy. I don't have to get up so early in the morning now. Next week we leave for Brazil. I will send you a space-card from there. I can't wait to go on holiday.

By the way, I am sending you the latest news about the monster – I hope you like it!

Anyway, I hope you will spacemail me soon. I am looking forward to hearing from you.

Your friend
Darius

Location: London, England
Planet: Earth
Date: 11th November 2287

Dear Zmod

I'm just sending you a quick message to see how you are. It's strange not to hear from you for so long - I hope that nothing is wrong.
Let me know because I'm waiting for your news!

Your friend
Darius

Location: London, England
Planet: Earth
Date: 21st November 2287

Hi Zmod

I still haven't heard from you. Are you OK? Please let me know!

Your friend
Darius

The English Times

3rd December 2287

Disaster on Bartoch as Dormant Volcano Erupts

After lying dormant for over one thousand years, the Arqiat Crater volcano in the country of Bozkin on planet Bartoch erupted in July with tragic consequences for the inhabitants.

Following an imposed news blackout by the Bartochian authorities, nothing was known of the situation for four months, but thanks to an emergency mission to Bartoch last week by the World Council envoy, Dr Sabrina Elahi, details are beginning to emerge. According to figures she gleaned from communications with the Mind Complex, which governs Bartoch, over 800,000 people are either dead or missing and around 2 million have been made homeless.

"The capital of Bozkin, Vakpak, has been totally destroyed by the eruption of the volcano," said Dr Elahi. "The devastation and the suffering of the people is profoundly shocking."

The eruption of the volcano has angered people in Bozkin, and many have accused the authorities of not having done enough to protect people from the disaster. Others have demonstrated against Dr Elahi's visit stating that they do not want outside interference.

> "We were always told that the Arqiat Crater posed no danger to us!" said one angry resident. "Because of the complacency of the Mind Complex, I've lost half my family and I have nowhere to live. My whole life has been destroyed. Now your people are coming over here to take advantage of our plight. We don't want you here."
>
> Dr Coree Mundu, an eminent Bartochian vulcanologist agrees. "The Mind Complex has failed and I don't know why they are turning to you for help. Not long ago, I warned that the Jellibech Springs area was a disaster waiting to happen but certain people chose to rubbish my claims. What we don't want now is outsiders complicating the situation."

Location: London, England
Planet: Earth
Date: 3rd December 2287

Dear Zmod

I've just read terrible news about the volcano in Bozkin erupting. I hope you and your family are OK. Please let me know. I am really worried.

Your good friend
Darius

Darius logged onto the Members section of the Inter-Galactic Space Club site. He had some spacemails from his other penfriends, but he did not really care about them. He was looking for a reply from Zmod, but yet again there was the familiar rejection message:

'Error 134i: Message not delivered. Unrecognised spacemail address. Please try again or contact your club representative.'

Darius couldn't understand it. This was at least the tenth time that his spacemail to Zmod had not been delivered by the computer. He had called the Space Club's office and they had told him that to their knowledge there was nothing wrong with the Bartochian teleconnection. They did not know anything about the volcanic eruption. Now he didn't understand what was going on and he didn't know what to do! Did this mean the end of his friendship with Zmod? This disaster suddenly made him realise how important his relationship with Zmod was. He wished he could have told him so.

Location: Nihotepec, Tarzak
Planet: Bartoch
Date: 18th Girion, Hexile 14785

Dear Darius

I am sorry that I haven't spacemailed you for such
a long time, but we had a terrible disaster in Bozkin.
As you can see I am now living in Tarzak at my aunt's
place.

Maybe you have heard on Earth that the Arqiat
Crater volcano near Jellibech Springs erupted. No one
expected it! I was walking back from school with my
friends when it happened. The ground started to shake
and the air began to get very hot. Suddenly, before
we could do anything there was a huge explosion and
rocks began to fly through the air. The people around
us began to run and we followed them. I didn't know
where we were going but I knew that something very
bad was about to happen. As I looked back I could see
buildings on fire and I could hear people screaming.
Molten lava was flowing down the tunnels towards us
and the ground began to get covered in ashes. Smoke
was everywhere and I lost sight of my friends. I was
sure that I was going to die. It was horrible. The air
became very hot and it made it difficult to breathe.

I suddenly saw a bus and I tried to reach it. The driver
slowed down slightly but didn't dare stop. Fortunately,
some of the passengers on board opened the door and
told me to run towards it. As I did, they caught hold
of me and dragged me into the bus. They told me that
the volcano had erupted and was destroying the city. I

wanted the bus to head towards my home, but the bus driver said that it was impossible. He said that it was too dangerous. Even as we drove, every few seconds we heard explosions, followed by rocks hitting the roof of the bus. Some of the passengers started to scream because one rock smashed the back window and made the bus swerve. Luckily the driver somehow managed to keep the bus on the road. I tried to look at what was happening outside but it was almost impossible to see anything. There was so much dust in the air that the sky had turned from green to black.

The bus driver took us out of the city to a town called Tengip on the other side of Bozkin. At Tengip, the situation was crazy. All I could see was police trying to hold back big crowds. We were taken to a hospital and left in a waiting room. I kept trying to ask the hospital staff about my family but they said that they could not help me. They were running around trying to attend to the wounded people that were being brought in. It was complete chaos in the hospital and I was very scared.

We waited in the room for several hours before anyone came to see us. Eventually a policeman arrived and told us that we were going to have to stay in the room for that night until the situation was under control. He said that they were having a lot of problem evacuating people from Vakpak because the eruption had destroyed most of the city and lava was blocking the roads. They could not fly into the city because there was no visibility for aircraft. He told us to write down our names on a form and that he would try his best to find out where our families were.

We stayed in the hospital for three days. It was

really frightening because I didn't know if my family had managed to escape from Vakpak in time. I was afraid that I might never see them again. No one seemed to have any reliable news and there were a lot of rumours flying around. The hospital staff tried to help us, but they were very busy because there were so many emergency cases to deal with. Quite a few times, I saw people with burns being wheeled on trolleys through the corridor to the operating theatres.

I really began to give up hope of seeing my family, but one day when I was in the dining room waiting for a meal I saw a familiar face. One of the nurses, who was also there recognised me and came over to see me. She worked with my mother in Vakpak Central Hospital and told me that all medical personnel had been called up for duty as soon as news of the volcano had erupted. She told me that she had working all hours of the day because there were so many injured people. Even though she was so busy she said that she would try to find out if my mother was in the hospital. Although she had not been on duty when the disaster happened, she said that she was fairly sure that anyone at Vakpak Central hospital would have escaped because it was not too close to Jellibech Springs. They would have been brought immediately to Tengip because it had been designated the central hospital for the region. Even though no one had expected the volcano to erupt the Bozkinian hospital system had a special procedure already in place for any national emergency.

I was so relieved when my mother eventually turned up. She was crying and it was very hard to speak to her. She told me not to worry about my father because he had not been near the volcano. As soon as he had realised what was happening he immediately went to his base. The base had special bunkers to protect the staff there and so he had been able to hide there. Then when it was possible he had flown to Tengip. Like the medical staff, all military personnel had been told to report to Tengip for duty. According to my mother, my father had gone with his unit back towards Vakpak to help with the rescue teams. She told me that she would put a call out to his unit to tell him that I was safe. However, she hasn't heard from my grandfather. We don't know where he is. We're really worried about him because he lives outside Vakpak.

My mother went to see some hospital officials and then they allowed me to leave the waiting room where I had stayed with the other passengers from the bus. My mother thanked them for rescuing me and told them that she would do her best to find out what had happened to their families.

Unfortunately, it wasn't all good news and it is probably why my mother seemed very nervous speaking to me. It was about Darak.

She told me that all that morning Darak had been going crazy inside the house, screeching a lot and bouncing all over the place. She said that it was almost as if he knew that something bad was about to happen. She tried to calm him down but nothing worked. He didn't even want to play with his favourite green rock. Later he began to get worse and so she decided to take him outside into the main tunnel. The strange thing was that he started to panic and bit her arm and dragged her outside! She couldn't understand what he wanted but he seemed desperate to get away from the house. He wouldn't let go of her arm and he became really angry when she wouldn't move quickly. She said that she actually started running because he was scaring her. Then she saw that the rocks on the side walls were beginning to split and lava was seeping out from the cracks. She started to scream and ran as fast as she could because the tunnel behind her was collapsing. She heard Darak screech very loudly and then go silent, but because of the dust she could not see where he was. She was picked up by a passing hydroskimmer and it was only when they were clear of the collapsing tunnels that she realised that Darak had been left behind.

My mother told me that he saved her life, but I didn't know what to say. I was very upset. I have had Darak since he was a pup and I don't want to think about him dying like that. He was my best friend and I don't know what I am going to do without him. He was always with me and now I feel like I will be lonely forever.

I'm very sorry to end this spacemail but I'm too sad to write any more. I wish all this had never happened. Everything has been destroyed in Vakpak and I don't even know what's going to happen. It's as if life will never be happy again for me.

I hope you will write soon. At least your spacemails might make me feel a bit better.

Zmod

Location: London, England
Planet: Earth
Date: 3rd May 2288

Dear Zmod

I was SO happy to hear from you!!! I was really worried because you had not answered my spacemails for a long time - I was sure that something bad had happened, and then I read this terrible article in the paper. It is a relief to hear that you and your family are safe. I was truly sorry to hear about Darak though. He sounded so funny! It is terrible news and I don't know what to say to make you feel better.

I read about the eruption of the volcano in our newspapers and saw reports on the news about it. It takes a long time for information to reach us from your planet so it was hard to know what exactly was happening on Bartoch. I did read recently that our planet's World War Council had voted to send an international rescue team to help with the disaster in Bozkin. I am glad that my planet is trying to help yours.

Please keep spacemailing me. You know that you are my friend. If there is anything that I can help you with, please let me know. Don't give up hope even if things seem very gloomy at the moment!

Your good friend
Darius

16th March 2291

Darius was excited. It was not every day that you received a visitor from another planet and yet that is what was going to happen to him today!

Darius had been writing to Zmod for over five years now and he was looking forward to actually meeting him. Over the years he had learned a lot about Bartoch from Zmod.

"Hurry up Darius," his father called from downstairs. "We mustn't be late."

Darius ran down the stairs and jumped into the hoverjet. In half an hour they were at the airport complex. Darius waited whilst his father went into his office to get a coffee and that is when he saw the space ship approach.

It was a large silver oval structure and with two cubical engines mounted on its side. It slowed in the air and then began to descend vertically. Once it was on the ground a door opened and a ladder automatically dropped to the ground.

Out stepped Zmod and his father. Zmod was exactly as Darius had thought. He was short, with dark skin, yellow eyes and green hair. Zmod also recognised Darius immediately and broke out into a broad smile.

'Finally we meet,' grinned Zmod. "I feel as if I already know you!"

"Me too!" replied Darius. "This may be the first time that we have met but I think that we are already best friends."

"What would you like to do today?" Darius asked Zmod.

"Anything," replied Zmod. "Absolutely anything at all."

About the Author

In moments of boredom, be they running on a treadmill or listening to lectures at yet another scientific conference, Faiz often found his mind beginning to wander into the mysterious realms of outer space. As circumstances for these explorations increased, he found himself creating the mysterious planet of Bartoch, inhabited by the friendly alien child called Zmod. In his first fiction book "My Alien Penfriend", Faiz looks at how Zmod's growing intergalactic friendship with a child on Earth reveals the darker secrets of his home planet. Faiz lives happily far away from Bartoch in London, England with his wife.

Printed in the United Kingdom
by Lightning Source UK Ltd.
109027UKS00001BC/2